ROBIN HOOD

Robin Hood

Based on Walt Disney Productions
full-length cartoon feature film

This adaptation by
Derry Moffatt

© Walt Disney Productions

FIRST NEL PAPERBACK EDITION APRIL 1974
Reprinted April 1974
This revised reprint May 1975

NEL Books are published by
New English Library Limited from Barnard's Inn, Holborn, London E.C.1.
Made and printed in Great Britain by Hunt Barnard Printing Ltd., Aylesbury, Bucks.

45002018 5

ye
colden

Chapter One

Who was Robin Hood? Was there a Little John? What *really* happened in Sherwood Forest, anyway? It was thought the answers had been lost with the passing years, but now at last, the animal kingdom has decided to reveal the true story as handed down by their ancestors.

But wait!

Before I tell you the story of Robin Hood I should introduce myself. I am Alan-A-Dale, a rooster with a yen for music. I play a mandolin and am called a minstrel. Because I can crow loudly too, it was decided by popular vote that I should unfold this strange tale.

Sherwood Forest lies in the county of Nottinghamshire. It still is a beautiful area and in those far-off days was heavily timbered, untilled and vast. That was where Robin Hood lived – in the heart of the forest. He was seldom alone for he had a band of merry friends . . . a group of animals who didn't take life more seriously than they had to. Not unless their most hated enemy, Prince John and his slippery side-kick, Sir Hiss

started making their greedy demands on the forest folk.

Robin Hood was a jaunty, courageous fox. His closest pal was Little John, a big, bumbling good-natured bear who hated bullies.

On the outskirts of the deep forest lay the city of Nottingham. It boasted a magnificent castle surrounded by a high stone wall. Inside this castle lived Prince John, the villain of this story. He was a mean, scrawny lion with a miser's lust for money. His down-trodden subjects lived in constant fear of his greed and displeasure. Amongst his wily, evil-tongued counsellors none was more hated than Sir Hiss, a slippery, oily tongued snake. Even those who lived within the protection of the castle walls quaked when the snake slithered into view. He could not be trusted at all, and the folk *outside* the castle, especially those who dwelt in the forest had good reason to fear him.

Sir Hiss made no secret of the fact that he got his kicks from creating misery wherever and whenever possible. When he slipped into his basket for a snooze he would dream of bigger and better tortures to inflict on defenceless victims. When he was awake he fawned over Prince John, whispering flattering remarks into his ear.

Sir Hiss had one 'special' hate . . . his old enemy, Robin Hood. He never lost an opportunity to use his venomous tongue against Robin and Prince John was a willing listener. Robin Hood was too popular with the poor folk and had to be watched. But the snake's vanity was at a low ebb. No matter how cunningly he had devised his scheme, Robin Hood had always bested him. Sir Hiss waited with impatience for the day he felt sure must come . . . the day when proud Robin would be publicly humiliated – and then killed. The snake chuckled maliciously, mentally visualising the scene. He would make sure that Maid Marion was present to witness the spectacle.

Maid Marion was a very cute vixen. Robin Hood had a big crush on her and was often teased by his friends about it. He took their jests with his usual good humour but hoped that one day he and the pretty female fox would be together. Meanwhile, Maid Marion lived in the castle chambers. Her constant companion and Lady-in-Waiting was a fat dowager hen, known as Lady Kluck. They passed their hours together strolling in the castle grounds, playing badminton and being entertained by the court jesters.

Secretly, Maid Marion longed to escape and live in the forest with Robin Hood and his friends. He was the most exciting fox she had ever met. Eagerly she listened to the court gossip for news of her lively hero for his name was often bandied about. It was only with the greatest difficulty that she concealed her delight at his victories over the unscrupulous Prince John and Sir Hiss.

Prince John had more than a passing interest in pretty Maid Marion. His presence caused her lovely red coat to bristle but she feared Sir Hiss even more. In him she recognised deadly danger for Robin Hood and it was difficult to feign half-hearted friendliness for her own safety.

On the day that my story begins, Robin Hood and Little John were strolling happily through Sherwood Forest. It was a warm, sunny morning and Robin Hood whistled as he brushed leaves from his Lincoln green tunic and breeches. Both he and Little John were unconscious of the fact that they were being stalked by the Sheriff of Nottingham, a fat evil wolf. With him was his posse of smaller, rather sullen wolves. Morose, they followed their leader, minds still dwelling on the breakfast the Sheriff had forced them to abandon. The Sheriff, a powerful personality in the city of Nottingham hated Robin Hood with a vehemence to match Sir Hiss and Prince John.

On this fine morning, one of the Sheriff's spies had informed him of Robin's whereabouts and the fat wolf lost no time in banding together the posse wolves. Robin Hood made a habit of robbing the rich to give to the poor. This was a well-known fact although Robin had never been caught. But a charge could always be trumped up. Now was the moment when Robin Hood was completely off-guard.

Little John looked down at his big, dusty feet. 'Say, Robin, let's make for the pool. I could sure do with a dip.'

'Right! I'll race you.' Swiftly, Robin took off, the bear lumbering after him.

They were frolicking noisily, splashing the sparkling water at each other when suddenly, Robin Hood spun round. His alert eyes had caught a movement behind a thicket.

'Quiet!' he warned Little John.

The bear stopped splashing, his arm still raised in mid-air.

At that moment the Sheriff of Nottingham let out a long howl of rage. 'They've spotted us. Come on. Charge! Don't let them escape or I'll lay a whip over your lazy hides.'

Snapping and snarling, the wolves raced towards the pool.

'It's an ambush. Quick . . . swim for it.' Robin Hood ducked under the water.

With a might lunge, Little John followed causing a great wave to smack the Sheriff's furry face. It sent him reeling backwards. In fury he kicked one of his posse, then baring his fangs plunged into the pool.

Emerging on the far side, Robin Hood and Little John dashed madly through the trees. 'Make for the Shambles oak' yelled Robin.

The oak was a special tree of huge dimensions. A concealed door in its trunk led into a partly hollowed centre. It always proved a good hiding place in desperate moments. Well ahead of their pursuers, they reached the Shambles. Little John, being anything but little, entered the secret door while Robin swiftly climbed the tree, concealing himself in the dense foliage. A tense minute passed before the breathless posse came into view. Through the leaves, Robin Hood could see the Sheriff's face contorted with hatred.

'Outwitted again. Darn their hides.' In a frenzy of rage, the fat wolf pawed the ground, then turning on his pack, swore at them and ordered a retreat.

Robin Hood waited until the posse were out of sight then descending from the tree's upper branches, gave a special rap on the tree-trunk's door. Little John emerged, his thick coat damp and matted, a cobweb covering one ear.

'Phew . . . that was a close one. Are you sure they've gone?'

'Yes.' Robin Hood laughed merrily. 'You should have seen

the Sheriff's face. His posse are in for a rough ride.' With another chuckle he flung himself on the ground.

'If it's all the same to you, I'd feel safer if we were hidden,' said Little John. 'Let's *both* climb the tree and keep a look-out.'

'All right, old pal – if it's going to make you happier.'

Settled on a high but sturdy branch, Little John rubbed the cobweb from his ear. 'How many times do I have to ask Sally Spider not to spin her webs so low,' he complained.

Robin craned his neck, ignoring the bear's grumbles. 'The coast looks clear. I don't want to sit up here for long.'

'The trouble with you,' said the bear fixing Robin with his brown eyes, 'is that you don't take this situation seriously. If we'd been caught . . .'

'But we weren't.'

'Robin, what do you think? Are we good guys or bad guys – y'know, robbin' the rich to feed the poor? In a sense, we *are* breaking the law.'

Robin patted his friend's big paw. 'But it's an unjust law and after all, we only borrow a bit from those who can afford it.'

'You're right, Robin – like always. If only we could get rid of that imposter, Prince John . . . Hullo, what's that?'

Through the forest resounded a loud fanfare of trumpets.

'Yippee! It sounds like an answer to what I've just been saying. Another collection day for the poor.' With a smile of happy anticipation, Robin Hood used his vantage point to see what was passing through the forest. In the distance he made out a heavily guarded coach. 'It's someone very important . . . might even be Prince John himself. I've an idea . . . but we must disguise ourselves.'

'Disguise ourselves . . . what as?'

'Gypsy fortune-tellers. People love having their fortunes told. I've a box of tricks hidden in the Major oak across the clearing.'

Chapter Two

The royal coach thundered through the forest. Animals ran from its path to hide behind protective trees. Inside, Prince John was laughing, his cruel face creased and ugly. On the plush seat beside him lay a pile of gleaming gold coins and his crown.

Greedily he scooped the coins up with his hands. 'Taxes, taxes, taxes,' he exclaimed. 'Beautiful, lovely taxes.'

Seated opposite, Sir Hiss snickered. 'No one is as clever as you, Prince at squeezing money from the people. Ooooohh... I love to see you in action. You're a genius.'

Leaning across, the Prince patted the slimy snake and guffawed even louder. 'Right! No one can outsmart me. Rob the poor to feed the rich ... that's my motto.'

The snake's slimy grin widened. 'You excel yourself. Not like your foolish brother, King Richard ... always trying to help the poor and needy.'

'I'm glad we managed to get rid of him,' said the Prince reaching for his crown and placing it rakishly on his mangy

head. Whenever his brother Richard – stately regal lion – was mentioned, the Prince felt insecure. True, he and Sir Hiss between them had foiled Richard with a clever plot. But Richard was very popular with his subjects and if the truth came out, there would be a revolt. The people were rebellious now but so cowed with fear at Prince John's savagery they were afraid to risk an uprising. Meantime, they suffered . . . and waited for the noble King Richard to return from his duties far away.

Sir Hiss felt very clever. It was he who had used his powers of hypnotism to send King Richard to the crusades, leaving the coast clear for Richard's unscrupulous brother John. This mysterious power had proved invaluable to Sir Hiss and got him in solid at the castle. He had no intention of losing his position as chief counsellor unless it was to climb *up* the ladder of fame. It paid him to fawn and toady to his master, although he often despised the scrawny lion. The Prince had an explosive temper and at times, Sir Hiss was the indignant victim.

This morning however, the greedy Prince was happy. He and Hiss laughed uproariously over the tricked King Richard until the snake unwittingly said 'Yes . . . he's vanished to our joy – but much to the sorrow of the Queen Mother.'

At the word 'mother' a remarkable change came over the tatty lion. His face fell and he started to sob, 'Mommy, oh mommy,' then vigorously sucked his thumb.

Sir Hiss could barely conceal his contempt at the Prince's odd behaviour but nevertheless he welcomed such weakness. It gave him yet another hold over him.

In the meantime, behind the major oak, Robin Hood and Little John were hurriedly donning their disguises.

'Say, how do I look?' enquired the bear as he struggled to tie an apron round his expansive middle. 'Aww . . . I can't reach.'

'Let me help.' Robin Hood tried not to explode with mirth. His fat friend looked very comical in a brightly coloured cotton dress and a kerchief tied beneath his chin. 'You eat too much honey,' he told the bear. 'Here's some fleece from Letty the Lamb's coat. Use it for curls, the finishing touch.'

'It's all right for you,' grumbled the bear good naturedly, 'you're smaller than me and can climb into things faster.'

'Yes . . . including mischief,' laughed Robin slapping Little John on the rump. 'Hurry . . . there's no time to lose, the coach is almost here.'

The two happy bandits took up their position on the pathway, a basket at their feet, wares held tantalisingly aloft.

'Look,' exclaimed Prince John who had by now mopped away his tears. 'There are two gipsy women by the roadside. Stop the coach and see what they have to offer.'

'Be wary,' warned the more cautious Sir Hiss. 'They might be bandits.'

'Foolish snake,' scoffed Prince John. 'Who ever heard of *female* bandits? What rubbish!'

The royal coach came to a sudden halt smothering Robin Hood and Little John in a cloud of dust. With feigned humility they stepped forward.

'A humble good morning, Prince John,' commenced Robin Hood. 'Buy some trinkets from a poor old gipsy woman and I will tell your fortune and bring you luck.'

Prince John thrust his heavily jewelled hands through the coach window. 'Very well, miserable crones. You have permission to kiss the royal fingers.'

Boldly, Robin Hood raised the Prince's hand to his lips while neatly managed to slip one of the rings from his middle finger. His action though swift, was noted by the still highly suspicious Sir Hiss. The snake hissed an audible warning into his master's ear. But Prince John, annoyed by Hiss's ticklish tongue firmly grabbed the slippery snake and tied a knot in his throat.

'That will teach you to interfere,' he growled. 'Respect your betters who know more than you.' Seizing a basket from the floor of the coach he stuffed his luckless councillor inside, slammed down the lid and then sat on it. 'Suspicious creature,' he snapped before returning his attention to Robin Hood.

'Climb inside the coach, gipsy and tell my fortune. I'm warning you, it had better be good.'

Without further ado, Robin did the Prince's bidding. Closing the curtains of the royal coach he whispered, 'Close your eyes and concentrate.'

. Uttering mysterious incantations, Robin Hood called on the mighty spirits to enter and reveal the future. Outside the coach, Little John was waiting for his cue. At Robin's words, he thrust a 'crystal ball' through the curtains. In reality, the crystal ball was a glass globe filled with fireflies. Little John dangled it from invisible string tied to a stick. It looked most effective.

'Ah . . . the spirits are favouring us today,' purred Robin Hood throatily. 'Open your eyes . . . the evidence is before you.'

The unsuspecting Prince gasped in surprise. 'Incredible,' he shouted. 'Amazing! Real floating spirits,' In his excitement, he jumped up and down on the snake's basket.

'You must keep your eyes on the crystal ball,' warned Robin Hood. 'We must not displease the spirits,' Even while he was speaking he was reaching for a sack of gold close to the snake's basket. Through a tiny gap in the basket's side, Sir Hiss was watching. His tail reached out and slapped Robin's hand away.

'What's going on?' demanded Prince John. 'You are disturbing my concentration.'

'Relax,' replied Robin. 'It's all part of the ritual.' Momentarily calmed, the Prince sat back, engrossed again by the crystal ball.

Outside the coach, Little John had not been wasting time. He had fixed the stick holding the glass ball in position, then expertly removed the solid gold hub caps from the coach wheels. On the roof, a heavily chained and padlocked chest had caught his eye. Swiftly, he bored a hole through it. A wealth of gold coins flooded out. With a joyous cry of 'Jackpot' he let the gleaming cascade flow down inside his huge bodice.

'The spirits are about to throw back the curtain of the future,' droned Robin Hood inside the coach. 'But to learn these mighty truths, Prince John, you must first remove your shoes and clothing.'

Too excited to question this odd request, the lion started to undress. As he struggled out of his shirt, Robin Hood hastily passed the sack of gold coins through the coach window to the grinning Little John. Then with a mighty 'Yippee' he leapt from the coach. Without pause, the lovable bandits beat a hasty retreat not stopping to even look back. Behind them they could hear screams of rage amid mortification, as the Prince yelled.

'Robbed!' he cried out. 'I've been robbed. After them, fools. You'll all pay for this.'

The coachmen who had been resting in a forest glade rushed forward and boarded the coach. But as they gave chase, the wheels fell off. Prince John and Sir Hiss who was still imprisoned in the basket were spilled into the dirt.

Prince John, completely frustrated and looking idiotic in just his underwear, beat the ground with his fists, tears of fury streaming down his cheeks.

'Let me out . . . let me out,' Hissed the snake.

The unhappy lion undid the clasp on the snake's basket. With a cunning smile the trapped creature slithered into the roadway. 'I knew it,' he said. 'I knew it, I warned you – but oh no . . . you wouldn't listen . . . '

'Shut up,' said Prince John furiously. Reaching for a hand mirror which had spilled from the coach he struck Sir Hiss vigorously on the head with it, shattering it completely.

'Now see what you've done,' whined Sir Hiss. 'Seven years bad luck you've brought upon us. Besides, you've broken your mother's mirror.'

The word 'Mother' again triggered off Prince John's strange reaction. Plaintively he began to both sob and shout 'Mommy . . . oh, mommy.' Then flinging himself on to the ground he sucked his thumb.

Back at the castle, Prince John, a mean lion at best, lost no time in seeking revenge. He had been publicly humiliated, losing both money and valuables. The story of his robbery had spread amongst his subjects and he had become a figure of fun. The Sheriff was summoned immediately and given his orders. Taxes were to be doubled, even trebled. The squeeze was on.

The Sheriff was a big, bumbling oaf but he excelled at one

thing and that was collecting money. He could smell – yes, and even hear it. What was more, he enjoyed his job and made a bullying game of it. Without further ado, he commenced his rounds.

The first call was at the home of an aged cobbler and his wife. They were owls named Tawny and Goldie. It was Tawny who spied the Sheriff approaching with his band of wolves. He screeched a warning to his wife – but too late. She was in the act of hiding all they possessed, two pennies, when the Sheriff burst in, and wrenched the money from her. Desperately she pleaded with the fat wolf but to no avail.

'Press on lazy curs,' shouted the Sheriff to his pack. 'We've lots more collecting to do.' Rubbing his hands in glee he turned his back on the distressed owls.

'It's no use,' said Tawny trying to comfort his sobbing wife. 'If we hooted all night we would still be mocked. Nothing will soften the Sheriff's hard heart.' Gently he led Goldie into their shabby little room, shaking his wise old head in despair.

The Sheriff's next stop was at the local village blacksmith, a hound-dog named Henry. He was of a naturally happy disposition but at the moment business was poor. Henry had a broken leg. It was in a cast and it was only with the greatest difficulty that he could manage to hobble about. A friendly sparrow had warned him of the Sheriff's intended visit. Henry, dejected and desperate, decided to hide his meagre savings in his leg cast. It was he felt, a unique hiding place. But to his dismay, when the wolves pounced and started searching, one of them knocked against him. Poor Henry fell over and the coins chinked.

'Ha,' bellowed the wily Sheriff, 'you'd best hand over that loot instantly, hound-dog, or you will have *two* broken legs.' Henry had no alternative. With a trembling paw he extracted the money which was immediately snatched. Howls of derisive laughter greeted his anguish. As the wolves retreated he lowered himself sadly into his one rickety chair and muttered, 'If only Robin Hood could help! Whatever shall I do now?'

Next on the cruel Sheriff's agenda was a visit to a family

of rabbits. Mrs Rabbit had been busy baking a carrot cake for it was her eldest son's birthday.

When the wolf and his pack burst in she was leading the young bunnies in a birthday chorus. Proudly, the boy rabbit held out his present for all to see – a whole farthing. The Sheriff grabbed it and when the bunny started to cry, patted him consolingly on the head.

'Don't take it so hard, Sonny. Prince John wishes you a happy birthday, too.' Then to his pack. 'No point in hanging about here . . . these rabbits never have anything except more rabbits.'

The corrupt band went on their way leaving tears and heart-ache behind them. At that very moment, a blind beggar tapped his way into the house. 'I'm so weary,' he said, 'and hungry too, could you spare a poor old man a bite to eat?'

Without hesitation the mother rabbit replied, 'We've very little to offer but you are welcome to a slice of carrot cake.'

With a gay laugh the beggar cast aside his stick and threw off his disguise. It was Robin Hood.

'Oooohhh . . . it's Robin Hood, our hero,' spluttered the birthday bunny, hastily drying his tears.

The welcome visitor was quickly surrounded by the entire family and they gulped out their tale of woe. The jaunty fox listened, his face serious. Slipping his hand inside his tunic he withdrew some gold coins and gave them to Mrs Rabbit.

Her face wreathed into smiles. 'Bless you, dear Robin. Whatever would the folk in Sherwood Forest do without you?'

'I hope they never have to,' he bantered. 'And now, it's your turn.'

Turning to the birthday bunny he gave him a bow and arrow for a present. The youngster was speechless with joy. His brothers and sisters gathered round in admiration.

'Here, have my hat as well,' insisted Robin, placing it on the rabbit's head.

'Thank you, thank you, it's the very best birthday I've ever had.'

'The hat's too big,' observed his smallest sister.

'That's all right,' assured Robin. 'He will grow into it with time.'

'Outside to play – all of you,' insisted Mrs Rabbit, to her excited offspring. 'I want to talk to Robin.'

With happy squeals her brood ran from the house.

'Just watch me,' said big brother. Taking a dramatic pose he drew back the bowstring. The arrow flew through the air in a high arc and disappeared.

'Oh . . . oh dear . . . now you've done it,' yelled one of the younger bunnies. 'It's gone over the castle wall into Prince John's grounds. You've lost it.'

'No I haven't,' said the boy rabbit, very upset. 'I'll get it back – somehow.'

Jittery but determined he made his way to the castle walls. The other youngsters held back watching with apprehension. Finding a grilled fence let into part of the massive rocky wall, he turned to wave to his brothers and sisters then disappeared through the grill.

Chapter Three

Bitsy, for that was the boy rabbit's name, didn't feel half as brave as he pretended. Cautiously, he made his way through the undergrowth. His heart was hammering in the noisiest fashion. Just ahead, he spotted the errant arrow. It was caught in a bush. But hark . . . what was that noise? He could hear voices, too. Sneaking nearer, he saw a badminton court where two ladies were playing a game. As they shuttled the badminton bird back and forth they giggled and laughed.

Bitsy recognised one of them. It was the lovely Maid Marion. Once she had passed through the forest near his home. He had watched her from behind a tree and thought her the prettiest creature he had ever set eyes on. Nevertheless it was wiser not to risk discovery.

Silently he reached for his arrow when – bang! something landed at his feet. Petrified, he remained motionless. But already, Maid Marion was leaning over the bush to retrieve her badminton bird. She came face to face with the scared Bitsy. It would be hard to say who was the more startled.

'Great heavens, Lady Kluck. Come quickly and see what I've discovered. A real cute rabbit.'

Lady Kluck joined her companion and fixed Bitsy with a stern eye. He panted heavily, hoping the guards wouldn't be called.

'Who does he remind you of?' asked Maid Marion mischievously.

Lady Kluck, playing up to her companion, feigned surprise and answered, 'But of course! Only the notorious Robin Hood wears a feathered cap like that!'

Bitsy sighed with relief. He knew now that he was amongst friends and had nothing to fear. 'Can I have my arrow back?' he asked. 'Robin Hood gave it to me for my birthday and . . . '

Noises in the undergrowth made him look round. All his brothers and sisters and even some friends were coming towards the little group.

'Hullo, Bitsy,' called out a bold rabbit. 'We waited by the grill then decided to follow in case you were in danger.'

'Well, I'm blessed,' said Lady Kluck. 'Since you're here, come on to the badminton court. It's not so cramped.'

The uninhibited youngsters, now completely at ease, flooded around Lady Kluck and Maid Marion.

'Is Robin Hood your sweetheart?' asked one precocious youngster.

'Are you going to marry him and live in Sherwood Forest?' asked another.

For a moment, Maid Marion looked pensive – a little sad. 'It's a long, long time since I last saw Robin Hood. He has probably forgotten all about me!'

'Oh no, he hasn't,' retorted Bitsy. 'How could he ever forget anyone as pretty as you! I'll bet he'll come courtin' in grand style. Why . . . he will storm the castle walls, fight all the guards and carry you off to Sherwood Forest.'

'Just a minute,' interposed Lady Kluck. 'You've a very vivid imagination for a young bunny, but you're forgetting one thing. What of Prince John?'

'That mean old Prince don't scare me,' said Bitsy with more bravado than he actually felt.

Lady Kluck answered severely. 'Well, we will see about that! I, Prince John, challenge you to a duel.'

'Oh dear,' said one of the bunnies.

'It's okay,' said another. 'It's only a "mock" fight!'

Maid Marion passed Bitsy a toy wooden sword. The fight was on. He attacked Lady Kluck with his sword. She retaliated with her badminton racket. They parried back and forth a few minutes to the amusement of the spectators. Finally, Lady Kluck, somewhat exhausted, grabbed Bitsy's wooden sword and pretended to plunge it into her bosom.

'I'm dying,' she cried dramatically. She fell to the ground amidst cheers from the bunnies and Maid Marion's laughter.

Bitsy felt concern. Was Lady Kluck really hurt? Leaning over he whispered, 'Say, did I hurt you? I didn't mean to but ...'

Lady Kluck opened one eye. 'Now is your chance to drag your Lady Fair off to Sherwood Forest,' she whispered.

'Gosh ... you've been playing games with me,' said a relieved Bitsy. Seizing Maid Marion's hand he rushed into a rose arbor surrounded by bushes.

'So *this* is Sherwood Forest. It's lovely! Maid Marion's eyes were dancing with laughter.

'What are we gonna do now?' enquired the rabbit.

'Well, I think you are supposed to give your Lady Fair a kiss!'

Bitsy was suddenly shy and embarrassed. 'Aw ... that's sissy stuff. I couldn't!'

'Of course you could ... but if you won't, then I will.' The irrepressible Marion leaned forward and deposited a kiss on the bashful bunny's cheek.

The other rabbits and Lady Kluck had drawn close and were watching. They broke into peals of happy laughter crying out, 'They're kissin'!'

'It's been fun,' said Maid Marion patting Bitsy on the head. 'But you'd best go now for the guards check the grounds every hour.'

'The rabbits gave squeals of concern and made for the grille in the fence. ' 'Bye, Maid Marion ... 'bye, Lady Kluck.

Thanks for a lovely afternoon.'

As Bitsy hurried through the undergrowth, he remembered to collect his arrow.

Later that same afternoon, Maid Marion and her companion were resting in their castle chambers.

'Cheer up, Marion, you look positively gloomy. What's the matter?'

'Playing with those rabbits brought back all my memories of Robin Hood. Oh, Kluck, I *do* love him so.'

'Remember child, absence makes the heart grow fonder!'

'Or forgetful,' sighed Marion gazing sadly from her high window. 'By now, he's probably forgotten all about me.'

In Sherwood Forest, Robin Hood and Little John were in the log cabin which they shared. Robin was bending over a cooking pot, his face thoughtful.

'I don't like it,' he said to the big bear. 'With this squeeze on, and Prince John being in dangerous mood, there's no knowing what might happen next. Even dear Maid Marion could be in danger!'

Little John was washing out his smalls. He squelched about in the huge puddle at his feet, his homely bear face concerned. 'See here, old pal, why don't you stop mooning around. Marry the girl!'

'I *do* love her,' replied Robin. 'She's the cutest, sauciest fox I've ever met . . . but she's a highborn lady of quality. What chance would I have with someone like her?' Gloomily, he stirred their dinner.

Little John flung his smalls over the clothes line. 'So . . . what if she has got class? She loves you, too. I'm convinced of it. Climb the castle walls and carry her off in style. She'll love you the more for such a deed!'

'But I'm an outlaw,' replied Robin. 'It's no life for her – me always on the run.'

At that moment, the cabin door opened. Robin Hood and Little John spun round as a very fat badger entered.

'Easy, fellas – easy! I've just dropped by for a friendly visit.'

'Oh . . . it's you, Friar Tuck. You're in time to join us for a meal,' said Robin.

'What a lovely sense of timing I have.' Friar Tuck, who was a *very* fat badger, gleefully rubbed his tummy. 'I couldn't help overhearing your remark,' he went on to Robin, 'about being an outlaw. For heaven's sake, son, that isn't so. Why, some day you'll be called a hero!'

Settling himself on a bench at the rough-hewn table, Friar Tuck chortled. 'Robin,' he began, 'I've brought you some interesting news. Prince John is holding an archery tournament tomorrow.'

Robin Hood was highly skilled in the use of the bow and arrow, indeed his amazing knack had more than once been called wizardry. He smiled at the badger's news. 'Little John and I can rest assured that invitations won't be coming our way.'

Slyly, Friar Tuck went on, 'No, but there's someone who *will* be looking for you, Robin.'

'Who is that – the Sheriff?' asked Robin with a laugh.

'Nope. It's Maid Marion,' answered the fat Friar. 'I have it on good authority she's gonna give a kiss to the winner.'

'Wow . . . what am I waiting for?' An excited Robin Hood turned to his friend. 'Don't just stand there, Little John – pack my arrows!'

'No, Robin – no!' Little John frowned. 'Forget it! The field will be crawling with Prince John's soldiers.'

'At such a time, who's considering the odds?' Robin Hood, eyes gleaming, had turned his back on the cooking pot and was already examining his arrows.

'It *is* risky,' admitted Friar Tuck. 'In fact, it could be downright dangerous. Best do as Little John says.'

'What lack of confidence,' retorted Robin. 'You know the saying, faint heart never won fair lady.'

'Let's eat now,' said the badger. 'Forget the tournament.'

Robin gave a loud 'whoopee'. 'Little John,' he said, 'feed that greedy badger so that he can shut up. I've got to think of a plan. This may be my greatest performance!'

Good natured Little John looked suddenly melancholy. 'Or your *last* one!' he retorted.

Chapter Four

In our first chapter, dear readers, I introduced myself as Alan-A-Dale, a wandering minstrel . . . and your story teller. I am proud to be named after an ancestor of mine – yes – another Alan-A-Dale! He lived in the adventurous days of Robin Hood and was happy to serve that merry fox and call him friend. My forbear played a lute . . . my mother says we've always been a musical family.

On the day of the archery contest my ancient relative Alan-A-Dale was with Friar Tuck in the tournament field. They were mixing with the crowds and keeping an eye open in case of possible trouble for Robin Hood.

Prince John and Sir Hiss were seated in the royal box. The scrawny lion was dressed in a red robe trimmed with ermine. His crown was awry, resting against one ear but he felt that he looked very grand. With a smug smile he surveyed the gathering crowds.

'Hiss,' he exclaimed, 'this is a red-letter day. A coup d'etat, to coin a Norman phrase.'

'Sire,' returned Hiss, 'You are so clever. Your plot to capture Robin Hood in public is *sheer* genius.'

Hiss was in his best fawning mood today, determined to curry favour with the unpredictable prince. Ever since the robbery in the forest the snake had suffered many indignities at the hands of his ruler. He had even been banished to the servants' quarters for three days. With his virulent ways he had at least succeeded in amusing himself making life unbearable for the already over-worked staff. When Prince John had sent for him to resume his role of court counsellor, the servants breathed audible sighs of relief. The cook had even been heard to mutter something about 'a snake stew for lunch'.

But today the sun shone and Sir Hiss felt on top of the world . . . as far as a snake could. 'Yes,' he smirked. 'Robin Hood won't outwit us *this* time.'

'Robin Hood! That blackguard! Every time I hear his name I want to explode. Ohhh . . . how I loathe him.' Prince John shook with rage pushing his crown to an even more lop-sided angle.

'Ahh . . . ' retorted Sir Hiss who wanted to keep the lion as good-humoured as possible,' here come the elephants. Twenty-four grey elephants in fancy trappings were approaching the tournament field. As they reached the gates, in unison they lifted their trunks and blew a mighty fanfare. This signalled the opening ceremony – the tournament would soon begin.

Not far off in a clump of bushes near the field, Robin Hood and Little John were donning their disguises. They knew without them they would be instantly recognisable. Robin Hood had decided to disguise himself as a stork. He was in good spirits as he struggled to alter his appearance. 'Think I'll get away with it, Little John?'

'You'd better,' muttered the bear. 'But I'll be watching developments from the best vantage point. I intend to "con" my way into the royal box.' He struggled into his costume – that of a royal Duke. 'This should impress Prince John,' he said.

'Very effective! You look more stately than the Prince.' As Robin talked he strapped on a fake beak. Little John began to laugh. 'Sorry, Robin, I can't help it . . . you *do* look funny.'

'Off with you,' retorted Robin. 'Remember to keep a straight face in the royal box – and look out for that treacherous snake.'

'Best of luck, Robin.' The big bear wiped his eyes with his hanky and lumbered towards the field entrance.

Gathering up his bow and arrows, Robin Hood followed at a distance making his way towards the contestants.

The crowds were dense now and Little John had to elbow his way towards the royal enclosure. When he finally reached it, his way was barred by a petty official – a huge toad.

'Let me through, you slimy creature or it will be the worse for you. Do you know who I am?' Little John adopted his best airs and graces and glared pompously.

'I have my orders . . . ' began the toad.

Hearing the commotion, Prince John looked round. Impressed by the bear's grand dress and airs he snapped, 'Thuggy, let the gentleman through. At once.'

Little John approached the prince with a courtly bow. 'Thank you, gracious sire. Underlings can be tiresome at times!'

'They can, but if they offend in my realm, they pay for it . . . I never forget an insult.'

Sir Hiss regarded the grandly dressed bear with suspicion and jealousy. He resented strangers in the royal box. 'And *who* are you, Sir?' he asked scathingly.

With a grand flourish, Little John made a courtly bow. 'Sir Reginald, Duke of Chutney,' he replied with dignity.

Prince John was obviously impressed. He beamed warmly patting the cushioned bench on which he and Sir Hiss were seated. 'You are welcome to join us, Duke. Here – have a seat beside me. Make yourself comfortable.'

In an aside to Hiss he whispered, 'A grand fellow, eh, Hiss? He *does* have style!'

Hiss glared at the intruder and ignored the lion's remark, but he moved closed to the Prince, not wanting the Duke to usurp *his* position.

But Little John's eyes were on the lion. 'Say! You can't get a better seat than this – the *royal* box! Thanks, Prince John.

You don't know how this warms my heart.' Heavily he lowered himself on to the bench. Immediately, there came a long, agonised yell from under his ample rear. He had sat on Sir Hiss.

With an apology, Little John pulled the crumpled, furious snake out from under him. It was too much for Sir Hiss. He spat his animosity, convulsed with rage. To make matters worse, Prince John was holding his sides as he roared with laughter.

'Oh . . . oh dear . . . ' guffawed the lion. 'That's the best laugh I've had today! Hiss, with you around, who needs a court jester?'

The snake smoothed himself, trying to muster his dignity. But before he could re-arrange himself on the bench, Prince John said, 'You might as well make yourself useful. Get out there on the tournament field and keep your snake eyes open for you-know-who.'

Ruffled and venomous, the unhappy snake slid away muttering angrily beneath his breath.

Another fanfare of trumpets signalled the start of the parade. The long line of archery contestants lined up ready to walk past the royal box. A ripple of excitement went through the crowd. Both the Prince and Little John leaned eagerly forward in their seats and the mangy lion licked his lips in anticipation. Robin Hood would surely be among the archers.

Meanwhile, Sir Hiss sliding through the crowd was looking for the best way to observe *everyone*. He spotted a vendor selling balloons and smirked. Yes, there was no doubt he was a clever snake and Prince John would be grateful to him yet. A problem was solved. Slithering towards the unwary vendor he wriggled his head inside a balloon which lay close to the ground; the rest of his length trailed out behind him.

Gathering in a long breath, Sir Hiss blew air into the balloon, which inflated it more. Seconds later snake and balloon rose gently into the air. The vendor's attention was diverted; he was selling balloons to three yelping puppies and didn't notice what was happening. Twirling his tail like the rotor blade of a

helicopter Hiss moved through the air. He was making excellent aerial progress and congratulating himself, unaware that he had been spotted.

Down in the field, Friar Tuck and Alan-A-Dale were keenly alert. Robin Hood must have the maximum protection. They searched the faces all about them until Friar Tuck's attention was distracted. A fly had flown right into his eye. Blinking rapidly he looked upwards and *that* was when he observed the wily snake.

He grunted a warning to Alan-A-Dale.

The minstrel patted the badger's shoulder. 'Good scouting, friend. That fly was really a blessing. We will keep our eyes on the crafty Sir Hiss.'

By now, the long line of archers were parading past the royal box. Robin Hood in his disguise as an ungainly country stork was at the end of the line. He gulped with pleasure when he spied Maid Marion. She had joined Prince John and was looking very pretty. As he drew level with her he took a flower from his hat and handed it to her. His eyes were ardent as he bowed and then winked.

Maid Marion gave a faint start. Shrewdly, she had penetrated the disguise of the jaunty fox. Without further emotion she smiled sweetly at Robin. 'Thank you, Archer. I wish you good luck.' She did not want to arouse the suspicion of Prince John who was close by.

Unfortunately, Sir Hiss who was floating slowly above the royal box had noticed the exchange of smiles between the two sweethearts. Immediately suspicious, he twirled his tail and moved closer to Robin Hood, following him on to the archery field.

The competition began. In the line of archers, Robin Hood found himself standing beside his old enemy, the Sheriff of Nottingham. The Sheriff had not recognised him and was looking scornfully at the ungainly and awkward bird. He was convinced he would have no problems in beating the ungraceful creature.

With a great deal of show, the Sheriff shot his arrow at the target. It hit very close to the bulls-eye. He laughed then bragged, 'Well, how do you like *that* shootin', Scissorbill?'

Robin smiled but didn't reply. Instead he took careful aim. His arrow curved gracefully through the air and hit the bulls-eye dead centre.

From the royal box, Maid Marion gasped with excitement. Little John, playing up to his role of the Duke of Chutney turned to Prince John. 'Hmmmm . . . that shot was nothing but pure luck, P. J.'

The cunning snake, still spying from his balloon was now above and just behind Robin Hood. He hissed with uncontrollable joy. There was no doubt . . . the stork *was* Robin in disguise. With a fast flick he spun his tail to get up flying speed. He must report his discovery at once. There was no doubt in his evil mind that Prince John would reward him handsomely for *this* day's work.

Fortunately for Robin, Alan-A-Dale and Friar Tuck had followed the snake's progress. The balloon's sudden flight towards the royal box alerted them both and confirmed their fears.

'Help!' said the worried badger. 'The secret's out. We must do something – fast!'

In a flash, Alan-A-Dale placed the feather end of an arrow on the string of his lute. Using the lute like a bow he took careful aim. With a loud 'twang' the arrow streaked upwards. It hit the balloon. There was a loud 'pop.'

Sir Hiss couldn't understand what was happening. One minute he had been flying through the air . . . now he was being hurtled at alarming speed towards the ground.

'Great shot, Alan . . . you got him.' Even as he was speaking, Friar Tuck was running frantically to catch the snake.

Alan-A-Dale was close on the badger's heels. Friar Tuck managed to grasp the slimy snake. 'We must find a good hiding place,' he gasped as he wrestled with the snake's frenzied contortions.

Alan-A-Dale looked about him quickly then grinned. 'I think I've got the answer. It's over there.' Quickly he walked towards a huge wine cask.'

Friar Tuck chuckled. 'Excellent! That should give him a

REWARD

10,000 INGOTS FOR THE CAPTURE OF THE OUTLAW ROBIN HOOD

head-ache . . . and a hangover.'

The snake's eyes widened in horror as he guessed his enemies' intent. 'Unhand me, you ruffians! he spat. 'Unhand me, I say! You'll pay for this. Help! Guards!' But his cries of protest went unheeded. The guards were in another part of the tournament field, their minds not on the safety of Sir Hiss.

Between them, the minstrel and badger stuffed the writhing, complaining snake into the bunghole of the wine cask. With a loud 'thwack' Friar Tuck slammed in the plug. The barrel was sealed. From inside, Sir Hiss's muffled voice could be heard pleading, 'Please! Let me out . . . I don't drink.'

The two conspirators laughed heartily. 'You do now,' called Alan-A-Dale through the outer walls of the cask. From inside came the sound of noisy gurgles.   'Phewww . . . that should keep him out of our hair – at least for a while,' said Friar Tuck. 'Now to see if Robin's safe. I hope he isn't having trouble with the Sheriff.'

'I'll be glad when this afternoon is over,' replied Alan-A-Dale retrieving his lute from the ground. 'I shan't feel safe until we're back in the forest. Then I can play a cheerful tune.'

Meanwhile, all the archery contestants had been eliminated except the stork and the Sheriff. Excitement was running high amongst the spectators. The ungainly stork, though a stranger, carried the sympathy of the crowd. The target was ordered to be moved back thirty paces. This would be the *final* test.

The Sheriff looked worried. Prince John would show deep displeasure if he lost to a mere stork. He glanced round and spied Nutsy – a villainous vulture and one of the wolf's dull-witted deputies. He beckoned the bird down from his tree perch. Quickly he whispered instructions into Nutsy's ear. As the bird prepared to take off the Sheriff warned, 'Remember what you're supposed to do, Nutsy. Don't goof it. Now, get going!'

With a noisy flapping of wings, Nutsy flew off and hid behind the huge target. Using his beak he bored a peep-hole through it. Anxiously he waited, peering through the slot.

The Sheriff drew his bow, took careful aim and shot his arrow. Its angle was too high but Nutsy was ready. He raised

the target slightly to a better angle. There were long drawn out
'Oooohhhss . . . ' from the crowd as the arrow scored a perfect
bull's eye.

The Sheriff looked at Robin Hood with contempt and
said 'Just try to beat that, ungainly bird.' Drawing back his
lips he exposed yellow teeth in a cruel laugh. His worries were
over. He was convinced he had won the tournament.

Determinedly, Robin Hood took his turn. With bow string
pulled back he sighted down the arrow's shaft. The wily
Sheriff wasn't taking any chances. He reached between the
stork's legs with his bow. Deliberately he hit the tip of
Robin's bow just as he was about to shoot.

Robin Hood's arrow flew skyward in a high arc. Following
its curve with his keen eye, Robin knew it wouldn't hit the
bulls-eye. Swiftly he pulled another arrow from his quiver,
inserted it into his bow and aimed upwards. His action was
very smooth and fast.

The second arrow gained on the misdirected one, hit its
feathered tip and deflected it downward. There was a moment
of suspense . . . a hush hung over the spectators. Then the
arrow hit the target dead-centre. The Sheriff's arrow was
forced out of the bulls-eye and fell to the ground. Robin Hood
was undisputedly the winner.

The Sheriff stamped the ground in a frenzy of rage.
Deafening cheers broke out amongst the crowds. Robin, delighted at his success, waved to them. He would be presented
with the trophy, a *golden* arrow – and he could claim a kiss
from his sweatheart, Maid Marion.

Already, the guard of rhinocerous had formed to escort him
to the royal box. But the unsuspecting Robin Hood was in
for a cruel shock. The thwarted, angry Sheriff had finally
penetrated the stork disguise. Nutsy, the vulture was hovering
close by and the Sheriff lost no time in sending him ahead to
warn the Prince.

Unaware of his danger, Robin presented himself at the royal
box. He was confident that his clever costume had fooled the
greedy, tyrannical lion. The Prince leaned forward, an evil
smile on his lips.

Robin Hood grasped Prince John's hand and shook it with vigour. 'Your Highness, meeting you face-to-face is a real treat. I've looked forward to this moment with impatience.'

The lion resented such bold and daring familiarity. He pulled back his hand saying 'Release the Royal fingers – immediately.' Rising to his feet he continued, 'And now you shall get what is coming to you. I hereby name you the winner – or more appropriately . . . the *loser!* Prince John slid his sword blade under Robin Hood's coat, ripping upwards and cutting the cloth. The stork disguise fell to the ground.

Robin Hood tried to run – but it was too late . . . he was trapped.

'Seize him,' yelled Prince John triumphantly. The rhino guards swarmed over the luckless Robin Hood. Within minutes he was bound in chains.

A great roar of indignation rose from the crowd. Prince John held up his hands for silence. 'I shall now give my decree.' Turning towards Robin Hood he said, 'Prisoner, I sentence you to instant death! Traitors to the crown must die!'

'No . . . no . . . no.' yelled the crowd passionately.

Robin Hood looked the lion in the eye. 'Traitor to the crown? That crown you are wearing belongs to Good King Richard . . . not to you!' Struggling to face the crowd he shouted, 'Long Live King Richard!' The people of Nottingham echoed the words, 'Long Live King Richard!' They surged even closer.

This show of loyalty caused Prince John to lose his temper. He beat down on a table with his fists shouting furiously, 'I am *King, King, King!*'

'No . . . No . . . No . . . ' yelled back the crowd.

'I'll have no more of this nonsense,' stormed the maddened lion. 'Off with his head! Take the prisoner to the block at once.'

'Oh no! My dear Robin,' Maid Marion's sobs rent the air as she buried her face on Lady Kluck's shoulder.

Robin tried to turn in her direction but was pulled roughly away to the headman's block.

Chapter Five

Robin Hood's position was desperate. Little John, frantic with worry searched his mind for an idea. He was shocked at this unexpected turn of events. If his beloved leader was to be saved, rescue must be imminent. But how? Little John was still in the royal box in his disguise as the Duke of Chutney. A reckless plan occurred to him . . . at least it was worth a try.

In the general upheaval and excitement, the bear slipped unnoticed behind the rear draperies of the royal box. Resolute, he waited.

By now, Robin Hood feeling beyond help, was being lead up the steps to the dreaded block. The executioner was waiting, a black mask drawn over his face.

Robin's thoughts turned to Maid Marion and he felt very sad. She had sobbed so bitterly when the guards led him away from the royal box. He hoped his friends would try to comfort her.

Meanwhile, evil Prince John was impatient for the execution to take place. He would be well rid of this meddlesome fox.

The people of Nottingham must be made to realise that it was he – the mighty lion who was all powerful. King Richard's name would be forbidden within the realm. It didn't concern the Prince in the slightest that his people despised and loathed him.

With a grand gesture the Prince raised his arm. It was the awaited signal. The watching executioner raised his axe. A ripple of fear and protest surged through the crowds, who were being held back by a heavy guard.

Then to everyone's astonishment, 'Stop! Stop!' ordered Prince John. 'Executioner, hold your axe!'

People exchanged glances of disbelief. The masked executioner paused, axe held in mid-air. Whatever had come over the lion to make him suddenly change his mind?

But the quaking Prince had no doubts. Beads of nervous sweat stood out on his forehead as Little John, concealed behind the royal draperies, pressed a dagger into his enemy's back. The bear spoke in soft, menacing tones. 'One call for help and you'll be dead before anyone gets near. Now tell them to release Robin Hood before I use you for a pin-cushion.'

Unable to resist, Prince John repeated, 'Release the prisoner.'

The Sheriff who had been standing close to the block, wanting to see the fox's head fall, moved forward. '*Release* the prisoner? But, Sire, you said . . .'

Lady Kluck rushed forward to the edge of the royal box. 'Can't you understand an order, you buffoon! You heard what he said. Release him, Bushel Britches, release him!'

The Sheriff shrugged angrily looking again in the direction of the Prince. The lion looked odd . . . almost sick. Yet his order had been definite. Sullenly, the Sheriff walked back to the executioner's block and helped unbind Robin Hood. There was something decidedly screwy about the entire situation.

Robin Hood could scarcely believe his good luck. He sprinted down the steps and Maid Marion who had rushed from the royal box, flung herself into his arms. They embraced tenderly, Maid Marion's face radiant with happiness.

'Robin, dear Robin,' she said, 'I thought I'd lost you.'

By now it had registered with the slow thinking Sheriff that he had better check the royal box. Prince John was standing in the same position looking decidedly unhappy. There was no sign of Sir Hiss and he seldom left the Prince's side. It was odd . . . very odd.

Stealthily, the Sheriff crept around the back of the royal box, then almost choked with rage. As he'd suspected, it was a trick. Little John was still holding a dagger at the Prince's back.

The fat angry wolf lunged forward. 'Why you . . . !' Quickly he drew his sword and swung it viciously at Little John. The bear ducked just in time. But by now, free of the menacing dagger, Prince John was shouting as he pointed to Robin Hood, 'Kill him! Kill him!'

The fight was on!

Maid Marion's safety was Robin's first concern. 'Run and hide,' he warned her. Grabbing a sword from a nearby guard he cleared a path for his sweetheart. The other guards attacked, but Robin held them off.

Little John, outraged at the turn of events, attacked the Sheriff, disarming him. Then he ran to help Robin. Even Friar Tuck and Alan-A-Dale were in the melee. Though outnumbered they held their own as they tried to beat a retreat.

Cowardly Prince John, by now out of the royal box looked fearfully about for a hiding place. Spying a giant wine cask he hid behind it.

The fight continued to rage growing fiercer each passing minute. Robin Hood caught sight of Maid Marion. She was struggling fiercely as one of Prince John's men tried to seize her. Without thought for his own safety, Robin Hood quickly climbed a pole, grasping the rope which extended to another pole. With a mighty sweep of his sword he cut it and swung in a long arc towards Maid Marion. His weight knocked the guard flying as he swept his surprised sweetheart up into his arms. They swung clear over their enemies' heads and landed in a pile of straw.

'Run for it' gasped Robin, 'make for the forest.' Breathlessly, they raced through the trees. By now, Little John had caught up with them. Not far behind were Lady Kluck, Friar Tuck and Alan-A-Dale. Puffing and panting they made good their escape. Behind them, groups of confused and bewildered soldiers swore and fought amongst themselves.

Prince John, still cowering behind the wine cask, saw Robin's escape. Seething with rage he started to shout, 'Hiss! Hiss! Where are you? You're never around when I need you!'

Hiss's hollow voice emerged from the wine cask. 'Coming, Sire – hic!' Prince John looked all about him, surprised and puzzled. He couldn't trace the source of the voice but he could still hear it. 'For I'm a jolly good fellow – hic – Sir Hiss is a jolly, jolly good fello-o-o-w.'

The lion put his ear against the wine cask. Surely his court counsellor wasn't *inside*. But further gurgles and outbursts of song convinced him it must be so. More incensed than ever, Prince John lifted the plug from the bunghole of the cask.

With a little 'plop' Hiss popped into view and swam zig-zag fashion across the surface of the wine. Totally unaware of what had happened on the tournament field and of Robin Hood's eventual escape he said gaily, 'Oh, there you are, P. J.' He giggled, then continued, 'Sire, you'll never guess, but the stork is *really* Robin Hood!'

In a frenzy of anger, Prince John turned on the blissfully happy snake. 'Don't refer to me as *P. J.* you insolent creature. You're drunk! Is *this* what I pay you for?'

'But, Sire, you don't understand . . .'

'I understand only too well.' Prince John grabbed the protesting Sir Hiss and tied him into several knots and threw him on the ground. 'Get out of *that* if you can, you stupid serpent!'

Chapter Six

Robin Hood, Maid Marion and their friends continued their frenzied dash for freedom. Not daring to look back they ran and ran until they were in the depths of Sherwood Forest.

'Oh dear,' panted a breathless Lady Kluck. 'How much further?'

'Not too far!' promised Robin. 'But the Sheriff is a stubborn brute and won't easily abandon the chase.'

'Do you think he will find us?' asked Maid Marion tremulously. 'I don't want to return to the castle – and Prince John – ever.'

'You won't have to if I have my way!' Robin Hood took Maid Marion's hand. 'Come along! I know a special place where you and Lady Kluck will be safe.'

'Oh, Robin, you are so brave . . . and so clever.' Maid Marion's heart swelled with pride. Yes, she told herself . . . he really was a jaunty handsome fox.

Deep within Sherwood Forest was a waterfall and a natural grotto. To Robin it represented safety for his friends. When he heard the music of the cascading water he stopped running. Friar Tuck skidded to a sudden halt and Alan-A-Dale bumped into him.

'Whoa there,' said the merry Friar. 'We can walk the rest of the way.' The little group clustered round, glad of an opportunity to catch their breaths.

'Can I hear running water?' questioned Maid Marion.

'Yes! It conceals a beautiful grotto and that's where we're heading,' replied Robin. 'Are you all ready to go on?'

'If it means I can collapse into a chair . . . or even on the ground then the answer is yes,' said Lady Kluck fanning herself vigorously. 'I was really built for comfort – not speed.'

The group, relaxed now, laughed uproariously. Lady Kluck *did* look dishevelled, her usually impeccable gown crumpled and grubby.

A few minutes later the small company were admiring the waterfall – a sheet of water falling straight down, resembling a shimmering curtain.

'It's beautiful,' breathed Maid Marion. 'Where is the grotto, Robin?'

'Follow me!'

The grotto, hidden behind the curtain of water, was shaped like a tunnel. Lady Kluck and Maid Marion kept close to their leader and after walking slowly through the shadowy cavern, found themselves in a magnificent glen. Splendid giant English oak trees spread their branches towards a blue sky. The thick, springy grass looked smooth as velvet.

Maid Marion sighed her admiration while Lady Kluck said, 'Why, you sly fox . . . this is more gorgeous than the castle grounds.'

Robin agreed but said, 'What's more important . . . You and Maid Marion will be safe here until such time as Good King Richard returns.'

Suddenly, from behind the massive oaks surged crowds of people. They were the villagers of Nottingham. Delighted at Robin Hood's escape, they had come to the lovely glen to celebrate. It was as yet, undiscovered by Prince John and the wily Sheriff so they felt safe.

'It's Robin,' cried someone. Suddenly the air was rent with rousing cheers. 'Hurray . . . hurray for Robin Hood.'

People threw their hats in the air, turned somersaults, patted Robin on the back, shook him by the hand. Friar Tuck beamed a huge smile and Alan-A-Dale struck up a gay tune on his lute.

'Let's have a parade,' yelled someone else. The cry 'parade . . . parade . . .' was taken up. The people began to form lines to create a victory parade with Robin Hood and a deliriously happy Maid Marion in the lead.

Bitsy, the 'Robin Hood' bunny was weaving through the crowds on wobbly stilts imitating a stork. Anything that his hero, Robin Hood had done, he wanted to copy.

Alan-A-Dale and Friar Tuck had thankfully flung themselves on the grass beside Lady Kluck. Alan was strumming a tune on his lute, Friar Tuck was humming.

Friar Tuck looked across at Alan with a grin. 'I've got it,' he said . . . How's this?' In a deep, melodious voice he began to sing:

> Prince John's a mangy lion
> With a flea in his ear,
> And a scrawny brown coat
> That's tatty from the rear!
> And though he struts about
> And acts very vain,
> He really is a joke
> With a mangy mane!

The two friends pealed off into laughter. The happy villagers soon took up the ditty and adding their own versions of the vain, tyrannical Prince whooped and romped in high glee.

Effigies of Prince John and Sis Hiss appeared in the large opening of a hollow tree. For Prince John's head there was a pumpkin; his crown, a battered cooking pot. Sir Hiss was fashioned from an old, stuffed stocking. The bunny family were having a wonderful time as they activated their caricatures like a pair of Punch-and-Judy characters. Groups of grinning youngsters gathered to watch the puppet-like figures.

Other children had formed their own makeshift orchestra out of any musical sounding article they could find. Combs, toadstools, turtle's shells and hollowed-out coconuts all came into noisy use.

Industrious women-folk had used fallen trees as trestle tables and an assortment of food and drink was provided.

Prince John could be mocked today without fear and Robin Hood could not have received a warmer welcome from the throng, even if he had actually been crowned King.

Dancing and merry-making continued far into the night. The sun had slid behind the trees before the first of the villagers departed. The bunnies and other forest folk, worn out with excitement, had fallen asleep at their play . . . toys and musical instruments abandoned. Weary mothers prodded and roused their youngsters, urging them home to bed.

When the last stragglers had departed, Robin Hood put his arm about Maid Marion. She leaned her head sleepily on his shoulder murmuring, 'It's been the most wonderful day of my life, Robin. I shall never forget it.'

Gently he kissed her – twice. 'One is my prize for winning the tournament,' he said. 'The other, because I love you.'

Lady Kluck clapped her hands delightedly. She had fully recovered from her earlier exhaustion and was not feeling a bit tired. 'Can't we keep the party going?' she enquired.

'Oh . . . no . . . no . . . ' groaned Friar Tuck. 'I've had it. Just let me sleep . . . anywhere!'

Alan-A-Dale chuckled good-naturedly as he put his lute on the grass. 'You shouldn't have been so greedy,' he teased. 'I saw you have *three* helpings of plum cake.'

Friar Tuck rubbed his tummy with a mournful expression on his fat face. 'Yes . . . and can't I feel it now!'

'It's time for the ladies to retire,' intervened Robin. I've arranged a comfortable place for them to rest in the grotto. There, they will be well concealed and safe.'

'And what about us?' enquired Friar Tuck.

'We will go to our secret hiding place in the forest. Plans must be made. Prince John and that crafty Sir Hiss will lose no time in planning vengeance for my escape.'

The following morning, the bumbling Sheriff presented himself at the castle. The fat wolf was clutching a large bag containing taxes collected from the poor villagers. He had squeezed a little extra from a family of squirrels and hoped it would appease Prince John. He did not expect the lion to be in a very good mood after the tournament.

Sir Hiss was slithering across the floor of the receiving room when the Sheriff entered humming a tune.

'That's very catchy, Sheriff,' said Hiss. 'What is it?'

An ugly grimace crossed the wolf's evil face. 'It's about his Nibs, Prince John,' he answered. Everyone in Nottingham is singing it this morning. Listen!'

The Sheriff in his raucaus voice sang a verse of the uncomplimentary song made up by Little John the previous afternoon.

Hiss was amused and wriggled with pleasure. 'That's him to a T,' he laughed. 'Let me try it.'

Hiss commenced to sing the words with gusto. He hadn't yet forgiven Prince John for tying him into a series of knots the previous afternoon. The process of freeing himself had been long and extremely painful. His pleas for help had been ignored.

So the snake unleashed his venom in song. Suddenly, his attitude changed. He appeared to choke on his words. His keen eye had caught sight of Prince John, who unnoticed by either the Sheriff or Hiss, had entered the room. The lion was now seated in a high-backed chair, his head cocked forward in a listening attitude as he tapped the arm of the chair in menacing fashion.

Hastily the snake gulped and attempting to worm out of a difficult situation altered the words of the verse he had been singing.

> Prince John's a clever lion,
> And always very just,
> We're proud to be his subjects,
> He has all our trust!

The Sheriff scratched his ear in perplexity. 'Say, Hiss,' he said, as yet unaware of the Prince's presence, 'you've got it all wrong. It goes like this!' The wolf started to sing the correct – uncomplimentary – words.

'Enough!' Prince John's scream of rage made even Sir Hiss leap in fear. The lion leapt from his chair and advanced on his two cowering counsellors. His face was a mask of fury as he beat the air with clenched fists.

The slow-witted Sheriff blundered even further. 'But, Sire, it's a *hit* tune. Everyone in Nottingham is singing it!'

Contempt crossed the lion's ugly features. 'Including you – you wretched fool! Well, the people will be singing a *different* tune from now on. Double the taxes! Triple the taxes! Quadruple the taxes! Squeeze every last drop out of those insolent peasants!'

'But, Sire,' said the trembling wolf, 'I can't get more, I've already had everything they possess.'

'Don't stand arguing with me,' yelled the Prince. 'They pay – or go to jail!' To further emphasise his words, he grasped Sir Hiss by the neck and squeezed hard.

Desperately, the snake squirmed and wriggled until the angry lion flung him upon the floor. Peevish and sullen, Sir Hiss slithered quickly out of sight.

Prince John's wrath was soon felt by the luckless villagers of Nottingham. Unable to give that which they didn't possess, they were clapped into jail. Ruthlessly, the wolf did his job. He relished inflicting suffering upon his fellow-creatures and took sadistic delight in listening to their pleas for mercy.

The Sheriff's posse of wolves were kept busy rounding up whole families . . . and giving chase to those who tried to escape into the refuge of Sherwood Forest. The jail was full to overflowing. Even children were chained in dark, dank cells. Their situation seemed hopeless. The jail was impregnable, built of stone many feet thick. A heavy guard of Prince John's rhinoceros were on constant patrol.

Even Alan-A-Dale had been taken prisoner. As he looked sadly through the heavily barred window he shook his head.

'These are terrible days,' he muttered. 'Nottingham is in deep trouble.' Because he was a minstrel he was considered one of the fortunates – if *anyone* could be so called under such miserable conditions. He had been allowed to keep his lute and was not chained to the stone walls of the prison. This was because the guards demanded music . . . bored by their long hours of duty. It also helped to soothe the crying, unhappy children.

At the moment, Alan-A-Dale was in mournful mood. He strummed on his lute, singing a doleful song of Nottingham's dreadful plight. Gloom and melancholy was all about him and he thought longingly of Sherwood Forrest – and freedom.

Not far afrom the jail was Friar Tuck's church. The Friar was ringing the church bell though he knew better than to expect a congregation. Most of his flock were languishing in the city jail. Those fortunate enough to still be on the outside either hadn't been captured . . . or had paid out their life savings to keep their freedom . . . at least for a while.

No one was willing to risk attending church. The wily Sheriff could be lying in wait, ready to pounce. Friar Tuck hoped the bell would bring a ray of hope to his suffering friends. If only Robin Hood could come up with some daring plan of escape . . . but even to the usually optimistic Friar, it didn't seem likely.

The day was dreary and rainy . . . water dripped through a hole in the church roof. There was no money for repairs. Friar Tuck's tiny helper and church sexton was a mouse. He was seated at the organ playing on the primitive instrument but the music sounded sad and hollow in the empty church.

Friar Tuck sighed and walked sadly to the collection box for the poor. He lifted the lid and peered inside. 'Look,' he said to the mouse, 'our poor box is like the church – empty!'

The church mouse climbed down from his stool and scampered away to his mouse-sized room in the floor. Lifting back the mattress on his tiny bed he took out a single farthing. Then he trotted back to Friar Tuck.

'Times are bad, Friar Tuck,' he said, 'but Mrs Mouse and I . . . well, we've saved this.' He help out the coin. 'It's not much, but please take it for the poor. At least we still have a roof over our heads.'

Friar Tuck took the proffered coin. 'What a considerate creature you are. Your *last* farthing. No-one can give more than that!' He dropped the coin through the slot of the poor box.

Just then, the Sheriff's booming voice disturbed the brief, pleasant moment. 'Well,' rasped the wily wolf, 'I dropped by just in time.' Striding down the ailse of the church he stopped at the poor box. He lifted the lid and removed the coin. Even a farthing was a find as with practically everyone in jail his pickings were very poor.

Boiling with rage, Friar Tuck tried to conceal his wrath, but he couldn't help making his feelings known. 'Sheriff, that's the poor box!'

'It sure is,' chuckled the evil wolf, 'and I've just emptied it for poor Prince John.'

'Get out of my church!' cried Friar Tuck. 'You vile, unfeeling creature.' With his ample stomach, the Friar bumped the Sheriff backwards towards the door. 'Out!' he yelled with every bump. 'Out! . . . Out! . . . Out!'

In his indignation, Friar Tuck made the mistake of stepping beyond the church porch. The Sheriff's deputy, a skulking vulture named Trigger, swooped down from the limb of a nearby tree. With his cruel beak he pulled the cowl of Friar Tuck's robe over his head. The Sheriff snapped an iron manacle around Friar Tuck's neck.

'You're under arrest for high treason to the Crown!' shouted the Sheriff.

Friar Tuck was led off through the rain to jail. Inside the church, the little mouse stood wringing his hands in despair, tears streaming down his cheeks.

Chapter Seven

Inside the castle, Prince John was in a surly mood. He sat slumped in his chair staring into the empty fireplace. For days he had been brooding over the elusive Robin Hood. Where was he? Guards had scoured the city and forest without success.

Sir Hiss was seated opposite the Prince, out of arm's reach. Aware of his master's dark, sullen mood he didn't want to risk being tied into knots or half squeezed to death. He approached the lion cautiously. 'Sire, if I may venture an opinion, you are not your usual cheerful, genial self.'

The Prince growled without looking up.

Hiss tried again. 'Your Majesty, taxes are still pouring in . . . the jail is full. And, oh yes, I have *really* good news. Friar Tuck is in jail.'

Suddenly aroused, Prince John jumped to his feet exploding in anger. 'Friar Tuck! Idiot . . . miserable fool . . . it's Robin Hood I want!' In furious frenzy he tugged at his unkempt mane. 'I'd give all my gold . . . yes . . . all my gold if I could just get my hands on . . . did you say Friar Tuck?'

'Y-y-yes, Sire,' answered Hiss weakly, wishing now he hadn't ventured into the Prince's presence.

Prince John's crafty eyes lit up. 'Hiss, I've got it! Yes . . . by jove . . . that's it. I'll use the fat Friar as bait to trap Robin Hood. Friar Tuck will be led to the gallows in the village square and . . .'

'The gallows?' Even Sir Hiss's voice held concern. 'But . . . but, Your Majesty, would you hang Friar Tuck – a man of the church?'

'You dare to question my judgement? *I* rule this kingdom. *I* give the orders.' Prince John strode back and forth in determination. 'Yes, my repulsive, reluctant reptile, I *would* hang Friar Tuck! When our elusive Robin Hood hears of this measure, he will attempt to rescue the corpulent cleric. But my men will be ready . . . and there will be a *double* hanging!'

Prince John laughed heartily for the first time in days. 'Fetch the Sheriff' he ordered the snake. 'I want my plan put into operation at once!'

Hastily, Sir Hiss slithered away, not at all sure that the Prince's diabolical plan would work – yet not daring to further voice his opinion.

The first phase of Prince John's plan to capture Robin Hood was put into effect almost immediately. After an audience with the Prince, the Sheriff of Nottingham had a gallows built in the village square. The people in jail heard the hammering and rumours started flying. All trembled in fear. What new horror was about to descend upon their bowed heads?

When the gallows was almost ready, the Sheriff with his two deputies, Trigger and Nutsy tested it, making final adjustments.

Trigger, the ugliest vulture, hopped about in excitement. 'Sheriff,' he cackled, 'it's one of the smartest, prettiest scaffolds you've *ever* built!'

Nutsy, the slow-witted deputy flew down from his perch on the scaffold's upper beam to venture his opinion. 'Sheriff, don't you reckon we ought to give that trap-door a test? We wouldn't want it to fail at the critical moment . . .'

'Okay . . . we'll do that in a minute,' replied the Sheriff

who was standing right on the trap door.

But stupid Nutsy didn't wait. Instead, he grasped the trip lever and pulled down. The trap door fell open and the Sheriff, with a howl of rage dropped through the square hole. The upper half of his fat body remained wedged above the opening.

'Help! Get me out of here . . . you fool! Trigger flew off for assistance while the Sheriff sighed in resignation. Nutsy sat on his perch blinking in surprise. 'Now I know why your mother named you Nutsy,' he yelled at the bird.

At that very moment, Robin Hood, disguised as an old blind beggar was tapping his way towards the scaffold. He called out in a quacking, tremulous voice, 'Alms . . . alms for the poor.' He knew he couldn't hope for any assistance but he used his blind beggar's disguise to come into the heart of Nottingham to gather information.

As yet he was unaware of the fate that awaited his dear friend, Friar Tuck. Coming level with the scaffold, Robin enquired in a brittle, old man's voice, 'What be going on here, Sheriff?'

The Sheriff who was by now being assisted from the trap-hole, snapped, 'if you're blind, how come you know it's me?'

'Because I recognised your voice,' replied Robin.

'Oh!' replied the Sheriff. 'Well, it's pretty famous in these parts, I guess.' He struggled to his feet rubbing saw-dust from his breeches. 'If you really want to know what's going on, we've constructed a new gallows to hang Friar Tuck!'

'Hang Friar Tuck?' Shocked at this dreadful news Robin forgot to disguise his voice. Then catching the Sheriff's oddly questioning look he quickly recovered himself. 'Hang Friar Tuck, you say?' he quaked shakily.

Nutsy, still on his perch, answered, 'You betcha. At dawn! With luck, it will be a double hanging.'

Trigger flew across to his big-mouthed accomplice, flapping his wings furiously at Nutsy's beak. 'Shut up,' he screeched.

But Robin Hood had heard Nutsy's givaway words and realised fully what was meant. He played his part with admirable coolness. 'A double hanging, eh? And who be the other who gets the rope?'

Trigger flew across Robin's path jabbing his sharp bill in his direction. 'Sheriff, he's getting too darned nosey!'

'Oh, I didn't mean no harm,' asserted the beggar. 'But couldn't there be trouble if Robin Hood showed up?'

The dull-witted Nutsy made yet another goof. 'Well, what do you know . . . he's guessed it!'

'Nutsy, button your beak,' warned Trigger.

'No need to worry over anything I've guessed,' cackled the disguised Robin. He continued in a smooth, complimentary manner, 'The Sheriff be too crafty, far too clever and smart for the likes of Robin Hood.'

The clever words had the intended effect on the vain, strutting Sheriff. 'You hear that, Nutsy? For a blind beggar he sure knows a good man.'

'I'll be biddin' you gentlemen good-day,' croaked Robin. Taking care not to hurry or show concern, he tapped away from from the ugly gallows. Once round the corner and out of sight of the Sheriff and his vultures, Robin began to run in the direction of Sherwood Forest. He must tell the awful news to Little John. Something must be done . . . a plan devised if they were to rescue Friar Tuck and foil Prince John's wicked trap. There was very little time left. Already it was late afternoon; and tomorrow's dawn, the time fixed for the Friar's execution was but a few hours away.

Dishevelled and panting, Robin Hood arrived at the secret hide-out in the heart of the forest. Little John looked anxious when he saw his friend. 'What's wrong, Robin? Have you brought bad news?'

Quickly, Robin informed the big bear of the tragic events.

'It's even worse than we thought,' muttered Little John gloomily. 'If ever there was a time for desperate action, it's now. We've got to think of something.'

In the still, dark hours before dawn, Robin Hood and Little John stole cautiously into the City of Nottingham. Creeping forward they reached the high stone walls surrounding the jail compound and Prince John's castle. Dressed in dark clothes to help avoid detection, they peered about them. Wolves, armed with bows and arrows were doing sentry duty along the battle-ments.

'Where's Fang?' they heard one wolf ask. 'His post is un-manned!'

'Gone for a drink,' came the reply.

'Aww . . . I guess it's all right. The City's quiet as a grave tonight. We won't have any trouble.'

Robin Hood nudged Little John. This was their chance. Swiftly they scaled the wall at the point where the thirsty wolf should have been on duty.

Landing noiselessly in the jail's courtyard, they crept to-wards a shadowy archway. In the dim light the fat form of the Sheriff could be seen. He was leaning back in his chair beside the jail door, fast asleep. Only his deep, sonorous snores dis-turbed the still night air.

Robin Hood held up his finger in warning. His sharp ears had detected another sound. Trigger and Nutsy the two giant vultures were on patrol. Within a few feet of where they were crouching, Trigger passed by, his trusty crossbow, 'Betsy' at the ready. The two friends held their breath.

Nutsy, the dull-witted deputy, suddenly marched to the opposite side of the courtyard, did an awkward about face and stood like a sentry at his post. In a harsh, raucous voice he called, 'One o'clock and all's well!'

The tower clock immediately chimed three times. The Sheriff, awakened by Nutsy's loud voice, yelled impatiently, 'Nutsy, you'd better set your brain ahead a couple of hours.'

The dull bird scratched his head in puzzled fashion. '*Ahead*, Sheriff? Mmmm – now is that adding or subtracting?'

The Sheriff sighed with resignation. 'Aw, forget it, Nutsy. You're plain stupid! But how can I sleep with you yelling all the time. Shut up and get back to your sentry post.'

At that moment, Trigger appeared. 'What do you want?' snapped the Sheriff. 'Am I never to get any sleep?'

'Sorry, Sheriff,' replied the bird, 'but I've got an odd feeling in my bones like something's wrong. As if there's goin' to be a jail-break any minute!'

'Trigger, your imagination's working overtime.' The Sheriff

re-settled himself comfortably into his chair.

The suspicious vulture glanced about him doubtfully. As he strutted, the arrow in his loaded crossbow pointed directly at the Sheriff's nose.

'Point that pea-shooter the other way,' complained the Sheriff, by now thoroughly frustrated.

'Now don't you worry none. I've got the safety on old Betsy.' Proudly, Trigger patted the stock of his crossbow. With a loud twang the dangerously pointed arrow was released.

'Ouch!' The Sheriff ducked beneath the winged missile in the nick of time. 'What the heck are you trying to do – massacre me?' he exploded.

'I . . . I was only doing my duty, Sir.'

'You and that itchy trigger finger of yours,' shouted the irate wolf. 'Now get back to your patrol!' He aimed a vicious kick at the ugly bird who nimbly jumped out of the way.

'Preserve me from idiots,' muttered the Sheriff as he re-settled once again. He folded his arms across his bulging stomach and propped up his feet. 'Getting so a fellow can't sleep on the job anymore.' Within minutes, he was snoring again.

Nutsy felt fidgety and wished dawn would break. Night-duty seemed to go on for ever. He stomped across the courtyard and stood in front of a wall. Little John was concealed behind it. This was his chance. The big bear reached over and tapped Nutsy on the head. The bird looked up and was grabbed forcibly by his long beak and yanked over the wall. He let out a muffled cry of surprise which was hastily smothered. Robin Hood lost no time in effectively gagging the squirming bird. Then he tied him securely to a stout post.

The ever alert Trigger had heard Nutsy's one short cry. Alarmed, he shook the sleeping Sheriff, who looked ready to bite. Quickly, Trigger explained what he'd heard. 'Which direction did the noise come from?' By now, the wolf was on his feet.

Trigger pointed towards the wall. 'Over there,' he said.

'Then follow me.' Softly, the Sheriff padded across the courtyard. Trigger, trembling with excitement, his crossbow loaded and ready, crept close behind the wolf; so close that the tip of his arrow touched the Sheriff. The Sheriff stopped. 'Trigger,' he asked suspiciously, 'is the safety on old Betsy?'

'It sure is,' answered the bird confidently.

'That's just what I'm afraid of. After my near mishap, I prefer to follow *you*.' The Sheriff stepped behind the bird. 'Now proceed!'

Meanwhile, behind the wall, Robin Hood had been busy. Clever in the art of disguise, he had swiftly donned Nutsy's helmet and cape. A stocking pulled over his nose made it resemble Nutsy's beak. He waited his cue, cool and determined.

The Sheriff and Trigger explored the length of the wall, finally coming to its end.

'All right, you in there – come out with your hands up!' ordered the Sheriff.

'Yes . . . I've got you covered, too,' warned Trigger, aiming his crossbow.

Chapter Eight

Robin Hood flashed a quick look in Little John's direction, took a deep breath and stepped into view. Disguising his voice to sound like the slow-talking Nutsy he said, 'For Pete's sake, Trigger, put down that pea-shooter!'

The Sheriff gave a big sigh of relief. 'Aw . . . all this fuss and it's only Nutsy.' He turned back in the direction of his chair by the jail door. 'Relax boys,' he called over his shoulder. 'You've both got the jitters tonight.'

Trigger squawked in anger. He couldn't understand it. He was convinced that he'd heard something. He skulked off across the courtyard, peevish and sullen.

Robin Hood, thankful that his disguise had worked, followed the Sheriff back towards the jail. The Sheriff settled into his chair with a little sigh.

Determined to play the part of a good 'deputy', Robin lifted the wolf's legs on to a comfortable stool. 'You take it easy, Sir,' he said. 'I'll keep guard.' Softly he began to hum a soothing melody. After a couple of grunts, the Sheriff started to snore.

Tense minutes passed. Robin Hood bent over the sleeping wolf and with extreme caution slid the huge key-ring from his belt. The wolf slept on. Robin inserted the jail key into the door and turned it. There was a loud, metallic click. Robin Hood froze in horror as the Sheriff stirred. But with a snort his head dropped on to his chest. His snores continued. Robin pursed his lips in a silent whistle. Whew! That had been a close call!

From across the courtyard, Little John had been watching every move. When Robin motioned with his arms, the bear walked stealthily across the intervening space to join his pal. Together, they pushed gently on the jail door. It slid open and they stepped inside.

'Nice work, Robin,' said Little John. 'So far, so good!'

'Keep your fingers crossed our luck continues. Now you release Friar Tuck and the others . . . I'll take care of the royal treasury.' Robin gave the bear a reassuring pat on the shoulder, then headed for the Prince's tower.

Little John hurried along the dark corridors of the jail. They had a dank, nauseous smell and were poorly lit with spluttering rushes. 'Friar Tuck . . . Friar Tuck,' he called softly.

'Who wants the Friar?' said a tiny bunny who was cold, hungry and unable to sleep.

'A friend,' replied the bear.

'I'm glad someone's got a friend,' said the bunny. 'He's in a cell on his own at the end of this corridor.'

'Thank you, little rabbit. Be brave . . . you should soon be free!' Little John hurried on his mission.

Friar Tuck was standing with his nose pressed against the bars of his cell. In the dim glow of the rushes he had recognised his friend.

'I hope this isn't just a social call,' he joked.

Little John grinned as he selected a key on the huge key-ring. 'Oh yes. I make a habit of visiting friends in prison in the dead of night!' Quickly he unlocked the door.

Friar Tuck said solemnly, 'Bless you, my boy. I never thought I'd be so glad to see your homely face.'

'We must hurry,' urged Little John. 'Discovery could come

at any minute. I've keys to unlock the cells.'

'Marvellous! Where's Robin?'

'Gone to the Prince's quarters to look for gold. He intends to make sure the people won't starve once they're on the outside.'

Little John and Friar Tuck immediately set about opening the cell doors; then they unchained the prisoners. Many of them had been alerted and were overcome with joy. The tiny bunny had whispered Little John's message of hope to his mother and it had spread through the prison like wild-fire.

Everyone was warned to keep as quiet as possible. The major problem still remained . . . how to get them *all* safely out of the jail.

Alan-A-Dale, holding firmly on to his lute, looked through a jail window. He smiled and beckoned Little John over. 'What a fearless fox,' he whispered.

Robin Hood was climbing up the side of the tower of Prince John's castle. He had abandoned his cumbersome disguise and was using a long rope to pull himself hand-over-hand towards a balcony . . . the balcony of the lion's bed-chamber.

Reaching it safely, he climbed over its edge and peered through the window. A small light burned in the room. Robin could see a huge, ornate royal bed with a crown above it. On the bed, asleep and snoring loudly lay Prince John.

Sir Hiss was also asleep in a long, narrow bed that fitted his reptile body. All over the floor lay many bags of gold. 'Ah,' thought Robin. 'I guessed right. They guard it night and day!' He chuckled softly. 'Now to steal it!'

Realising that he would need assistance, Robin waved a white scarf in the direction of the jail.

'Look . . . a signal!' said Little John, breathing excitedly. Tearing off his own neckerchief, he waved back. Robin Hood, from the bedroom balcony, tied the end of his long rope to an arrow. With care, he inserted it in his bow, took careful aim and shot towards the jail. The arrow, carrying the attached rope, flew directly through the jail window.

Little John was ready. He knew what he had to do . . . that the gold – and Robin's safety was at stake. Grasping the arrow and rope, he threaded it through a large iron ring fastened to the stone wall. He then placed the arrow into a bow and shot it back towards Prince John's bedroom window.

Unfortunately, the arrow, pulling the rope behind it, shot straight through the Prince's window and hit the wall above his bed. Robin Hood suppressed a cry of dismay and dropped out of sight.

The Prince woke immediately, startled and alarmed. 'What's going on?' he muttered. 'If that vile snake is up to his tricks . . . ' But Sir Hiss was coiled up in his long bed fast asleep.

'Must have been a nightmare,' growled the lion softly. He slid beneath his bedclothes and dropped back into slumberland.

Robin Hood waited until he could hear Prince John's snores. Then he stepped swiftly from the balcony into the bedroom. Each bag of gold had to be tied on to the rope. It would serve as a long double clothes-line which could be pulled towards the jail. Friar Tuck and Little John would untie the bags as fast as Robin could send them across. The strongest of the villagers could carry them when they made their mass escape.

The clock tower tolled the hour. Robin paused to listen. It was four o'clock and would soon be dawn. He must work even faster. Desperately he seized one bag after another, taking care not to let the coins jingle.

Finally all the bags of gold but one were on their way across the courtyard. Robin breathed a deep sigh of relief. So far so good, he thought. After tying the last bag he seized the rope and gave the signal for his friends to pull him across to the jail too.

At that very moment, Sir Hiss awoke. It didn't take him more than a moment to grasp the situation. With a threatening spitting sound he reached up and, grasping the one remaining bag of gold in his mouth, pulled with all his strength.

Robin Hood, clinging desperately to the rope, was by now dangling helplessly above the jail courtyard. A frantic tug of war began; Hiss pulling from one end of the rope, Little John from the other. Robin felt like a yo-yo as he was reeled back and forth. Then a calamity threatening further disaster oc-

curred. The seam of a money bag directly over the head of the sleeping Sheriff began to split with the jerking of the rope. Another sharp jerk split it wide open. A steady stream of coins shot through the air and struck the Sheriff on the nose.

'Ouch! What the devil . . . ' The Sheriff looked up and saw what was happening. He opened his mouth to yell a warning, but his cry of alarm was stifled instantly. Friar Tuck slapped a large hand over the Sheriff's mouth and dragged him inside the jail.

Trigger, now recovered from his earlier tantrum, came flying round the corner of the courtyard looking for Nutsy. Instead, it was Robin Hood he saw dangling from the rope.

'A jail-break. I knew it . . . I knew it all along. Guards!' he began to shriek hysterically. 'Guards!'

Most of them had been asleep at their posts which was fortunate for Robin. They shot a steady stream of arrows at the brave but helpless fox but in the semi-dark their aim was not very good.

'I'm a sitting duck,' muttered Robin anxiously. 'Something had better happen – but fast!'

Sir Hiss, straining to hold the rope, wound his powerful tail around the foot of Prince John's bed. The violent tuggings and vibrations awoke the lion. With a maniacal growl of fury he leapt to the snake's assistance. 'Robbers . . . thieves,' he yelled. 'My precious gold . . . I mustn't lose it. I *won't* lose it!'

'Robin's in a very dangerous predicament,' said Little John to Friar Tuck. 'Muster the strongest men!' Willing hands pulled on the rope. The great combined weight was too much for Sir Hiss and the Prince. Robin and the remaining bags of gold shot through the jail window like a slingshot.

Both Sir Hiss and Prince John were pulled out of their bedchamber, across the balcony and dumped unceremoniously into the courtyard below.

The prisoners began to stream out of the jail, many of them holding bags of money. Prince John, bruised, battered and savage enough to kill began to scream. 'My gold! Stop! Stop! Where the blazes are the guards?'

Meanwhile, Robin Hood and Little John were making hasty

plans to organise the freed prisoners. They had to be led to safety . . . no small problem. All around was chaos, panic and confusion.

The rhino guard had been aroused and formed into a squad. Their commander shouted an order. Willy-nilly they charged forward. At a given sign from Friar Tuck the people ran sideways and avoided the onslaught.

Prince John and Sir Hiss were not so fortunate. The two of them were in direct line of the guards' flying feet. Still bruised and shaken from his drop into the courtyard, the lion had no chance to run clear. Sir Hiss already had a plan of action.

The Prince's eyes filled with horror as the rhinos galloped madly towards him. 'Hold it, you long-necked fools,' he roared. 'Hold it, I say!'

But it was too late to stop their great momentum. Cries for help were lost in the din and Prince John and Hiss were hit with the force of a bulldozer and carried forward. As the rhinos burst into the jail, Prince John's nightshirt caught on a great iron spike on the jail door. He was left dangling, helpless and crying with rage. Quick-thinking Sir Hiss had curled around one of the rhino's legs. It was a bumpy ride but at least he had avoided being stampeded to death.

Friar Tuck and Alan-A-Dale had discovered several large hay-carts. They were occasionally used to convey groups of prisoners from the City of Nottingham to the jail. Friar Tuck hoped to revise the situation and help the prisoners escape in them. Swiftly, they were filled to overflowing and the strongest men organised to push.

With cries of encouragement and a great 'Heave ho' from the men the carts began to move. Slowly they rumbled across the cobbled courtyard towards the main gate of the prison wall.

Robin Hood had managed to get clear of the guards. Grabbing a sword from an unwary wolf he cut the rope which raised and lowered the drawbridge. It crashed down with a mighty boom just in time for the first hay-cart to pass over the moat.

A group of wolf guards, running in single file, surged towards Robin Hood. With lightning swift accuracy he shot a succession of arrows at them. The arrows passed through the

hoods of the wolves' capes. Howls of fury burst from them as they were pinned to a wooden door at the end of the drawbridge.

As Robin dashed towards the moat he almost fell over a small bunny frantically calling 'Mama! Mama!' 'Come along, Floppy Ears,' said Robin pausing a moment to scoop the lost rabbit into his arms. 'We should find your mother on the outside.'

He continued his dash towards the main gate. Before he could pass through the large archway leading to freedom, an alert guard released a lever. The gate's heavy portcullis dropped down with a crash. The massive grating of iron bars had cut off Robin's escape.

Quickly he passed the squirming, terrified bunny through the bars to Little John. The big bear had just helped the last of the carts to safety. His face filled with concern at Robin's plight.

'Never mind me, Little John,' urged Robin. 'Take the villagers to Sherwood Forest and hide them. Hurry!'

Reluctantly the bear turned away from his friend. There was nothing he could do to help . . . and the people must be saved or be re-taken prisoner.

Chapter Nine

Robin Hood was alone and in great danger. Trapped, out-numbered and unarmed he could hear his pursuers' fast, pounding footsteps close behind him. Unable to run either to his right or left, he climbed the latticed iron bars of the gate. A dangling rope swung ahead of him. With his practised marksman's eye he jumped from the top of the gate.

From a dizzy height he swung on to a perilously narrow ledge of a high wall. Archers appeared over the crest of a roof-top and shot down at him. Arrows were falling like rain. Running along the precarious ledge he leapt across to the sill of a window, managed to pull himself up and disappeared through it. He was inside the castle.

Scarcely stopping to draw breath, Robin Hood dashed down a corridor. There was to be no respite. The Sheriff was barring his way. As Robin came into view, the Sheriff seized a lighted torch from its wall-bracket. He swung it with vicious force. Robin was just able to duck beneath the flames but he felt them singe the back of his neck.

The Sheriff, howling and snarling, made his next attack with a lance. Robin pulled a flagstaff from its standard and, using it like a lance, faced the raging wolf. A desperate duel began.

Flames were knocked off the still flaring torch. The sparks set the heavy draperies on fire. The flames licked savagely upwards. Robin darted up a winding tower stairway but the fierce fire cut off his escape.

The Sheriff advanced towards Robin with an evil grin. 'Trapped! Trapped at last! You won't get away this time!' He made a powerful lunge with his lance.

Robin leapt sideways. Flames were licking at his back. Escape looked impossible. With a mighty 'Woosh' more flames roared up the tower. They sounded like a chimney on fire. Smoke from burning wood and draperies drifted slowly upwards forming a dense cloud. Robin started to choke. To his left was a tiny window leading on to a high roof. Could he get through it?

With a mighty wriggle, Robin squirmed through the narrow aperture. He landed on the roof with a small bump. From inside the castle he could hear the Sheriff yelling, 'Surrender, you sly fox, before we *both* get burned. You can't win now . . . the game's up!'

'Not if I can help it,' thought Robin grimly. Below – *very* far below, was the deep water of the moat. It was the only way. Robin shut his eyes . . . then jumped. He plummeted downwards like a rocket, hitting the water with a mighty splash.

His battle for freedom was not yet over. As he surfaced, archers lined up at the top of the castle's parapet took careful aim. Their arrows splashed all about Robin as he swum valiantly for the opposite shore. He sank below the surface. Arrows continued to strike at the spot where he had submerged. Ripples on the surface of the water quietened – then disappeared.

Prince John and Sir Hiss, keen observers of Robin's valiant bid for freedom, looked expectantly at the smooth water. Tense seconds passed.

Then Robin's feathered hat floated to the surface.

Prince John clutched at Hiss and began to laugh hysterically.

'Hiss, we've got him! I can scarcely believe it. He's done for — finished!'

'Perhaps!' said the suspicious Hiss. 'Wait a little longer.'

The archers were congratulating themselves, already turning their backs on the moat. Behind a thick clump of bushes on the opposite shore, Little John had lain in wait for his friend. The carts carrying the escaped prisoners and led by Friar Tuck and Alan-A-Dale had managed to get clear of the city and were now deep in Sherwood Forest.

From his concealed position, Little John had watched Robin's brave leap into the deep waters. The deadly shots of Prince John's archers had made him fear the worst. Yet he had dared to hope . . . Robin Hood was a remarkable fellow.

But now he bowed his head in sadness. All hope was gone. How would he tell the others that there hero was dead? What of Maid Marion? She would be broken-hearted! Tears filled his brown eyes.

Then the kindly bear gave a surprised start. Moving towards him through the water was a hollow reed. It looked like the periscope of a submarine. The reed stopped right in front of the bushes. A sudden gush of water hit Little John's face. Robin Hood emerged smiling from below the water.

Little John smiled in wonder and relief. 'Robin . . . oh boy . . . you sure had me worried. Don't ever frighten me like that again! I thought you were a goner!' Leaning forward he helped his bedraggled friend from the moat.

'We'd best get away from this unhealthy spot,' said Robin, shaking the water from his coat.

'You said it!' agreed Little John.

Despite the night's hazards, the two friends sprinted like the wind. The deer of Sherwood Forest would have been proud of their efforts.

Their going, however, had not been unobserved. The keen-eyed Sir Hiss had spotted them. Prince John was laughing in high glee. Still clad only in his nightshirt he looked tatty and disreputable — but happy! 'Gone for good! Finished!' he chuckled, slapping at Hiss.

'You're wrong, Sire. He's fooled you. He's got away again!'

'No . . . no! He can't have!' The Prince followed the direction indicated by a smug Sir Hiss. When he saw that the snake was indeed right, he began to cry out with frustration. 'It's not fair! It's just not fair!' He began to whine and beat his fists upon the wall. 'I won't have it . . . I won't! Hiss, you're my counsellor. Tell me . . . what went wrong?'

Hiss snorted with disdain. 'Sire, your traps just don't work!' Then he said the very worst thing he could say to his irate master. 'Besides, look what you've done to your mother's castle!'

That did it!

Prince John, racked with sobs, shouted, 'Mommy!' Then he exploded in anger. Picking up a club he swung it viciously at Hiss. The snake slithered out of reach in an attempt to dodge the wild swings. 'You contemptuous cobra,' screamed Prince John. 'It's all your fault! Wait till I get my hands on you, you asinine asp!'

Chapter Ten

Three months had passed since the people of Nottingham had been rescued by Robin Hood and Little John from the castle jail. They had been happy, eventful months which had wrought many changes.

Prince John and Sir Hiss had disappeared – never to be seen again. Good King Richard had returned from the Crusades. The villagers, shedding tears of joy, had given him a rousing welcome. There had been celebrations and dancing in the streets. After cruel Prince John's tyranny, they could expect justice and good treatment from their *rightful* King.

As for the Sheriff, he had repented his wicked ways and thrown himself on the mercy of Good King Richard. The wily wolf had been given a final chance to prove whether or not he was capable of consideration. Now he knew better than to enforce his will except on wrong-doers.

Even Trigger and Nutsy, the two vultures, had pleaded to remain in Nottingham. They were still the Sheriff's deputies but their behaviour was polite, not raucous and sneaky as

Royal
Rock Pile

before. When the Sheriff heard he could retain the birds' services he turned to Nutsy with a grin saying, 'You're so crazy . . . who else would employ you?'

But now another *very special* day had dawned. It was Robin Hood's and Maid Marion's wedding day. Alan-A-Dale was strumming his lute as he beamed happily at a group of friends. Beneath shady trees, long trestle tables were laden with goodies for the marriage feast. Playful children darted about playing hide-and-seek.

Suddenly the air was filled with the merry pealing of church bells. 'That's it!' said Alan-A-Dale. 'We had better hurry over to Friar Tuck's church if we want to see the newly weds and wish them luck.

All of the villagers were crowded in front of the small church. As the doors swung open they gave a rousing cheer. Floppy Ears and Bitsy appeared first carrying baskets filled with sweetly scented flowers. The two bunnies threw the blossoms along the path. Then came the magic moment and the bride and groom appeared. Maid Marion was smiling and looked very beautiful. Robin Hood, smart in his Lincoln Green jacket and feathered cap beamed proudly at his lovely bride.

Cries of 'Good Luck!' and 'Best Wishes!' rang out from the merry throng of well-wishers. Robin and Marion waved joyfully as they walked the flower-strewn path.

The Sheriff, accompanied by Trigger and Nutsy were there too in their finest clothes. As the happy couple drew level with them the Sheriff commanded his two deputies 'Present – arms!' The birds stiffened to attention and raised their cross-bows. Accidentally, Trigger slapped the stock releasing an arrow. It sped through the air hitting the church bell with a loud 'clang'. Next it zipped down and sideways coming to rest in the centre of the colourful heart painted on the back of the marriage coach.

A roar of laughter went up from the crowd. The Sheriff turned to his deputies. 'I just can't rely on you two boys to ever do anything just right!'

'Aw . . . sorry boss,' said Trigger. 'Can I have my piece of wedding cake now?'

This was the signal for the celebrations to begin. Friar Tuck rubbed his tummy in gleeful anticipation as he looked at the laden table. Little Mr Mouse, his church sexton, teased, 'Don't overdo it, Friar or you will have a tummy-ache tomorrow.'

The Friar laughed good-humouredly. 'I'll worry about it when it happens,' he said, reaching for a large, sticky bun.

After the feast, goblets of wine were raised in a toast to the happy bride and groom. Alan-A-Dale and some of his friends had formed a band and there was dancing on the village green. The children played until they were too tired for more games. Their mothers began to gather them together to take them home to bed.

It was time for Robin Hood and Maid Marion to step into their coach. Across the back of it hung a huge sign that read 'Just Married'. Amidst cheers the couple waved their good-byes.

Robin took his bride in his arms. 'Do you know which way we're going?' Maid Marion nodded happily, as the coach moved along the road which lead through Sherwood Forest.

NEL BESTSELLERS

Crime

T021	548	GAUDY NIGHT	*Dorothy L. Sayers*	40p
T026	698	THE NINE TAILORS	*Dorothy L. Sayers*	50p
T026	671	FIVE RED HERRINGS	*Dorothy L. Sayers*	50p
T015	556	MURDER MUST ADVERTISE	*Dorothy L. Sayers*	40p

Fiction

T018	520	HATTER'S CASTLE	*A. J. Cronin*	75p
T013	944	CRUSADER'S TOMB	*A. J. Cronin*	60p
T026	213	THE CITADEL	*A. J. Cronin*	80p
T027	201	THE STARS LOOK DOWN	*A. J. Cronin*	90p
T017	524	MAGGIE D	*Adam Kennedy*	60p
T022	390	A HERO OF OUR TIME	*Mikhail Lermontov*	45p
T022	536	THE HARRAD EXPERIMENT	*Robert H. Rimmer*	50p
T022	994	THE DREAM MERCHANTS	*Harold Robbins*	95p
T023	303	THE PIRATE	*Harold Robbins*	95p
T022	968	THE CARPETBAGGERS	*Harold Robbins*	£1.00
T016	560	WHERE LOVE HAS GONE	*Harold Robbins*	75p
T023	958	THE ADVENTURERS	*Harold Robbins*	£1.00
T025	241	THE INHERITORS	*Harold Robbins*	90p
T025	276	STILETTO	*Harold Robbins*	50p
T025	268	NEVER LEAVE ME	*Harold Robbins*	50p
T025	292	NEVER LOVE A STRANGER	*Harold Robbins*	90p
T022	226	A STONE FOR DANNY FISHER	*Harold Robbins*	80p
T025	284	79 PARK AVENUE	*Harold Robbins*	75p
T025	187	THE BETSY	*Harold Robbins*	80p

Historical

T015	297	COUNT BOHEMOND	*Alfred Duggan*	50p
T017	753	WINTER QUARTERS	*Alfred Duggan*	50p
T021	297	FAMILY FAVOURITES	*Alfred Duggan*	50p
T022	625	LEOPARDS AND LILIES	*Alfred Duggan*	60p

Science Fiction

T016	900	STRANGER IN A STRANGE LAND	*Robert Heinlein*	75p
T017	451	I WILL FEAR NO EVIL	*Robert Heinlein*	80p
T027	279	DUNE	*Frank Herbert*	90p
T022	854	DUNE MESSIAH	*Frank Herbert*	60p

War

T027	066	COLDITZ: THE GERMAN STORY	*Reinhold Eggers*	50p
T026	299	TRAWLERS GO TO WAR	*Lund & Ludlam*	50p
T020	495	ILLUSTRIOUS	*Kenneth Poolman*	40p
T018	032	ARK ROYAL	*Kenneth Poolman*	40p

Western

T024	032	EDGE No 4: KILLER'S BREED	*George Gilman*	35p
T023	990	EDGE No 5: BLOOD ON SILVER	*George Gilman*	35p
T020	002	EDGE No 14: THE BIG GOLD	*George Gilman*	30p

General

T017	400	CHOPPER	*Peter Cave*	30p
T021	009	SEX MANNERS FOR MEN	*Robert Chartham*	35p
T023	206	THE BOOK OF LOVE	*Dr David Delvin*	90p

NEL P.O. BOX 11, FALMOUTH, CORNWALL.

For U.K. & Eire: customers should include to cover postage, 15p for the first book plus 5p per copy for each additional book ordered, up to a maximum charge of 50p.

For Overseas customers & B.F.P.O.: customers should include to cover postage, 20p for the first book and 10p per copy for each additional book.

Name ....

Address..

....

Title ....
(MAY)